The Dream Stair

The Dream Stair

BY BETSY JAMES

ILLUSTRATED BY RICHARD JESSE WATSON

HARPER & ROW, PUBLISHERS

Text copyright © 1990 by Betsy James
Illustrations copyright © 1990 by Richard Jesse Watson
Printed in the U.S.A. All rights reserved.
1 2 3 4 5 6 7 8 9 10 First Edition
Library of Congress Cataloging-in-Publication Data
James, Betsy.
The dream stair / by Betsy James ;
illustrated by Richard Jesse Watson.   p.   cm.
Summary: A young child's night is filled with wonderful experiences
traveling up and down the dream staircase.   ISBN 0-06-022787-7 : $
— ISBN 0-06-022788-5 (lib. bdg.) : $
[1. Dreams—Fiction.   2. Sleep—Fiction.]
I. Watson, Richard Jesse, ill.   II. Title.
PZ7.J15357Dr 1990   89-36420   [E]—dc20   CIP   AC

For Jan: a night-light
B.J.

For my son, my pal,
Jesse Joshua
(a.k.a. Astro)
R.J.W.

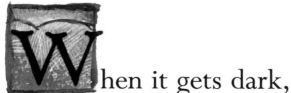hen it gets dark,
I go to bed
and my granny kisses me good night.
"Sweet dreams," she says.
"This candle keeps you
safe in the dark,
safe in my heart.
Go up the stair,
go down the stair,
and tell me all about it
in the morning."

She shuts the door.

So I leave me sleeping,
I take my granny's candle,
I open the door,
and there
is the old stair.

Up.

Up, up.

Past cupboards full of petticoats,
past cats and chimneys,

past balloons and trees.

Past pigeons.

Past clouds, past angels,
past blue air,
still on the stair,

until I come
to my attic room
with the white moon
at the window,

and there I play.

The moon rolls over.

Then I take
my granny's candle,
I open the door,
and there
is the old stair.

Down.

Down, down.

Past angels, clouds, pigeons,
past trees and balloons,
past chimneys,
past my own room with me sleeping,

down
    past kitchens, past halls,
    past cupboards full of spice,

past furnaces,
past roots,
past rivers running in the dark,

until I come
to my cellar room,
so dark and warm,
and there I play
until I remember day.

So I take
my granny's candle,
I open the door,
and there
is the old stair.

Up, up, up,
past rivers, past roots, past furnaces
and cupboards,
past halls and kitchens,
up the stair

until I come
to my very own room
with me sleeping,
and my granny's candle
always lit—
safe in the dark,
safe in her heart.

And I tell her in the morning.

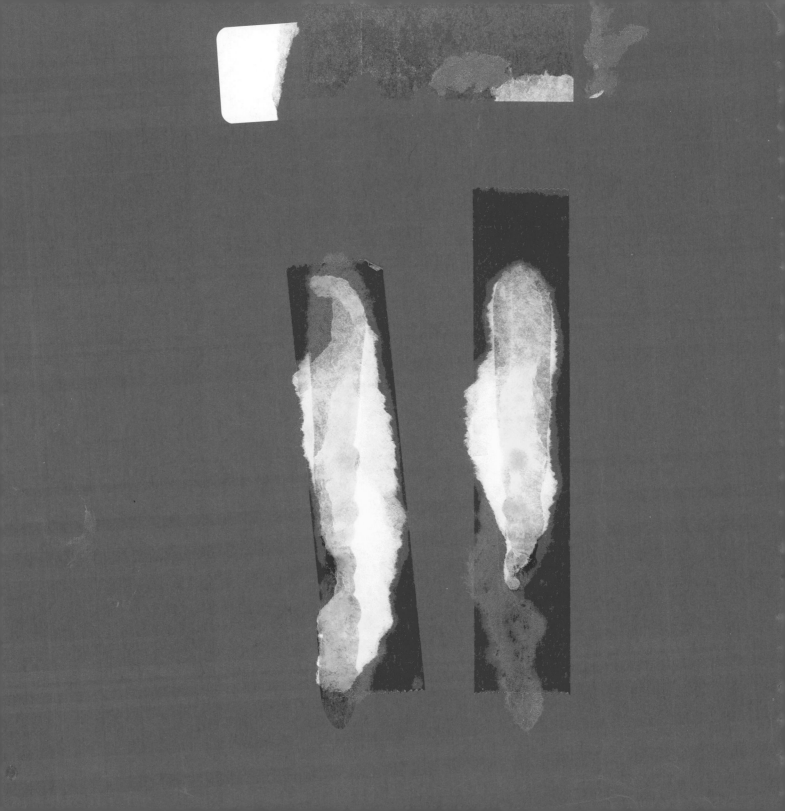